To Dean—my sweet boy who joins me on adventures both indoors and out

A Feiwel and Friends Book
An imprint of Macmillan Publishing Group, LLC
120 Broadway, New York, NY 10271 • mackids.com

Our books may be purchased in bulk for promotional, educational, or business use.
Please contact your local bookseller or the Macmillan Corporate and Premium Sales Department
at (800) 221-7945 ext. 5442 or by email at MacmillanSpecialMarkets@macmillan.com.

Library of Congress Control Number: 2022910212

First edition, 2023
Book design by Rich Deas and Matthew Cordell
This book was drawn with a 005 Micron pen and painted with watercolors.
Feiwel and Friends logo designed by Filomena Tuosto
Printed in China by RR Donnelley Asia Printing Solutions Ltd., Dongguan City, Guangdong Province

ISBN 978-1-250-31717-9 (hardcover)
1 3 5 7 9 10 8 6 4 2

PART · ONE

Magic Soup

Deep in Buckthorn Forest, at the northernmost edge of Burr Valley, high in the tallest red oak tree, behind the closed curtains of a bedroom window, hid a squirrel named Evergreen.

Evergreen was afraid. Afraid of loud noises. Afraid of meeting someone new. Afraid of heights, afraid of swimming, afraid of germs. And thunderstorms—her very worst fear was a thunderstorm! Evergreen was afraid of many more things than this, but it would take far too long to list them all.

But Evergreen was not afraid of soup. Her mother made the best soup in all of Buckthorn Forest, and everyone agreed this was true. Mama's soups were not only tasty—they were magic.

Mama's soups could make a cold person warm, a sleepy person awake, and a grumpy person happy. Mama's soups could even make a sick person healthy.

"Evergreen! I need you," called Mama from the kitchen.

Oh no, Evergreen thought. Anytime Mama said she needed her, it meant she was going to ask Evergreen to do something she was afraid to do.

"Granny Oak has come down with a terrible flu," said Mama. "This soup will help her feel better. Can you please take it to her?"

Evergreen thought about it for a second.

"No, Mama!" she said. "I can't do it!"

Granny Oak lived all the way on the other side of Buckthorn Forest; Evergreen had never traveled Buckthorn alone, and the forest could be a scary place— even if you weren't a squirrel named Evergreen.

"I'm sorry, Evergreen," said Mama. "But you must. Granny Oak is very sick. I have to stay here and make another soup for Auntie Maple's rash. I know you are afraid, but I believe you can do it!"

Evergreen did not believe she could do it.

But she put on her shawl and prepared to leave.

"Be very careful, Evergreen. Try not to spill a drop of this soup," said Mama.
She ladled it into an empty acorn and tightly screwed on the cap.
"Granny Oak will need every bit of it to get better."

Evergreen took a deep breath.

Then she went into the wilds of Buckthorn Forest.

PART • TWO

Briar

Evergreen made her way deep into the woods. Every so often, she would hear a noise and think, *Was that thunder?!*

So far it wasn't, thankfully.

But then, over a ridge, came a noise that was creepier and louder than any she had ever heard. And Evergreen was afraid.

"SKREEEE-EEE! Help!" cried a stranger—a fluffy white rabbit—trapped between two large stones. "I'm stuck! I'm stuck! And there are hawks in these woods!"

I . . . can't do it was Evergreen's first thought. Hawks eat rabbits. Hawks eat squirrels. Evergreen wanted to run. But what about the poor, sweet bunny?

She had to help. She had to try! Evergreen ran to the rabbit, and together they pushed and pushed and pushed until the massive stones moved apart. Evergreen's hands trembled. Her heart pounded. Until, at last . . .

. . . the rabbit was free!

"Thank you," said the rabbit, who introduced herself as Briar.

"You're welcome," said Evergreen, who introduced herself as Evergreen.

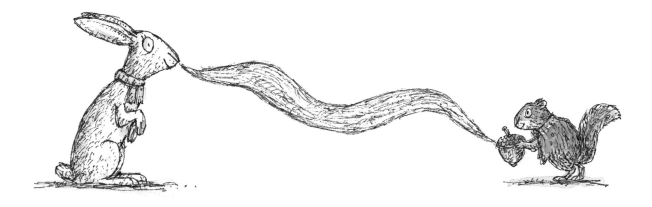

"Oh, my . . . ," said Briar, sniffing. "Is that soup I smell? Being stuck has made me so hungry . . ."

"Yes, my mama made it for Granny Oak. I'm off to deliver it now—"

Suddenly, the not-so-sweet bunny grabbed the soup and ran!

"Stop! Thief!" cried Evergreen.

And Briar did stop.

She looked up. She dropped the soup on the ground. Briar knew that bunnies weren't the only ones in Buckthorn Forest that went "SKREEE-EEE!"

Briar disappeared into the woods. Evergreen tried to hide, too, scooping up the soup along the way. But she wasn't fast enough to escape the red-tailed hawk—

—who snatched her up with razor-sharp talons and climbed into the sky.

Evergreen feared the worst.

SKREEE-EEE!
SKREEE-EEE!

PART · THREE

Ember

The wind whooshed as they flew.

The treetops blurred below.

Evergreen was afraid.

For a moment, she forgot she was carrying the soup.

She nearly dropped the acorn!

Whew!

Evergreen carefully plucked the thorns from Ember's back, wings, and breast. As she worked, she tried to explain her own dilemma—in case Ember reconsidered making a meal of her. She had to get Mama's soup to Granny Oak. Mama was depending on her!

Finally, Evergreen plucked out the last thorn.

"Ahhh . . . Thank you! I'm sorry to hear about Granny Oak," said Ember. "I will fly you there and make the journey quick."

"N-no thanks," said Evergreen, thinking better of hawks and heights.

"Fair enough," said Ember. "Perhaps we'll meet again, Evergreen."

Evergreen collected herself and then found her way back to the trail. *How frightening Buckthorn is*, she thought. And yet, she had rather enjoyed the adventure.

Before continuing, she stopped at a sparkling stream to have a drink.
When suddenly came another loud and terrible and ground-shaking noise.

"That's not thunder." Evergreen shivered. "It sounds worse!"

PART · FOUR

Sprig & Squirt

"Who's there?" croaked a toad.

"Whew," Evergreen sighed. Not thunder. "It's me, Evergreen, a squirrel."

The toad introduced himself as Grandpa Sprig.

"Forgive me, Evergreen. I'm an old toad, and I don't see too well," Grandpa Sprig said. "I wonder if you might be able to help. My great-grandson, Squirt, hopped out to that rock in the middle of Silver Stream. And now he's stuck—too afraid to hop back."

Evergreen could hop, but she was no swimmer. She might slip or be carried away by the stream.

Evergreen was afraid. But so was Squirt, who was alone and crying.

"I . . . can do it," said Evergreen.

"Thank you!" said Grandpa Sprig.
"And is that . . . soup I smell?" He licked his lips.

"Yes, I'm taking Mama's soup to Granny Oak,
who is sick with the flu," said Evergreen.

Grandpa Sprig licked his lips again.
I will take this soup with me, thought Evergreen.

The first two stones were easy to step across. And the next one, too. But the next stone was a big hop away.

Evergreen nearly lost the soup. And she almost fell into the water!

There was just one last long leap to Squirt's rock. *Uh-oh*, she thought. *I hope I make it.*

She made it!

Evergreen took Squirt in one arm and the soup in the other. And back they went to Grandpa Sprig. Crossing the stream seemed less scary the second time.

SPROING!
HOP! Hop!
step
step
step

Evergreen continued through Buckthorn Forest, encountering strange noises, meeting new friends, dodging a few enemies, and nearly losing the soup at every turn.

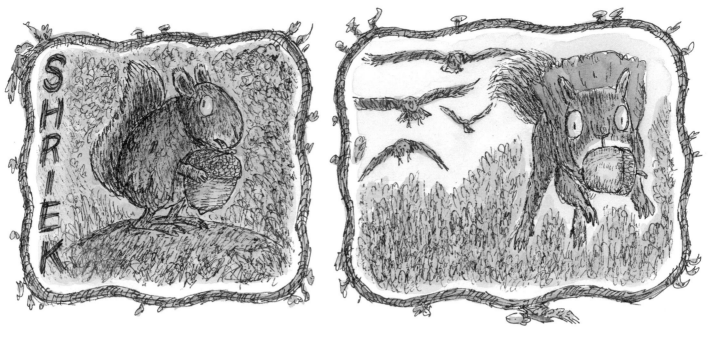

Evergreen was afraid, and yet . . .

She was happy.

Finally, she was there—Granny Oak's house was just down the trail.
And not a drop of soup had spilled!

But then came the loudest, scariest, ground-shaking-est noise of the day.

Evergreen's teeth rattled. Her fur blew back. She nearly toppled over.

She had to get Mama's soup to Granny Oak!

PART · FIVE

The Bear

AAAARRRRR!!

The cap of the acorn flew off! The soup sloshed, nearly spilling over the top.

"Oh no!" screamed Evergreen. "Granny Oak!"

The bear slumped to the ground and sighed.

"Granny Oak," said Evergreen, "you should not be out of bed in your condition. Mama made this soup especially for you." Evergreen screwed the cap back onto the acorn. "Let's get you inside."

Evergreen put Granny Oak back into bed and tucked her in. Granny opened her mouth, and Evergreen fed her every last drop of soup. It was still hot.

"Thank you, Evergreen," said Granny. "I'm feeling better already. You were very brave to come all the way here by yourself."

Evergreen smiled. She didn't say a word. Even if she agreed.

SKREEE-EEE!

SKREEE-EEE!

"I thought I'd find you here, Evergreen! Would you like
a ride home?" asked Ember.

Evergreen wasn't afraid.

"Yes, I would!"

And Buckthorn Forest looked much different on the way home.

PART · SIX

Home

Evergreen was excited to tell Mama about her adventure and all the animals she had met and the problems she had solved. She hung up her shawl and headed to the kitchen.

"Evergreen! I need you," called Mama.

"My brave girl! I knew you could do it!" said Mama.

"And you're just in time. Can you take this soup to Auntie Maple?"

"Yes, Mama," Evergreen said. "I can!"

She took the soup and put on her shawl.

CRACK!
BOOM!

"Sounds like a thunderstorm," said Mama.
"Best take an umbrella!"